Contents

Rachel Anderson

Carly's Luck

illustrated by

Harmen Van Straaten

First published in Great Britain in 1997 by Mammoth
an imprint of Reed International Books Limited
Michelin House, 81 Fulham Road, London SW3 6RB
and Auckland and Melbourne

ISBN 0 7497 3103 6

10 9 8 7 6 5 4 3 2 1

A CIP catalogue record for this book is
available from the British Library

Printed in Great Britain by Cox & Wyman Ltd,
Reading, Berkshire

1 The luckiest girl

AFTER SCHOOL WAS over, other people's mums were waiting to meet them at the gate.

And if not their mums, then their dads. Or their big brothers, or big sisters, or one of their aunties. Or their childminders, who stayed with them until their mums or dads got back from work.

Carly was different. There was never anyone to meet *her*.

These days she walked home on her own.

'It's not fair,' said Jasmin, who had to walk home with her nan. 'You can do just what you like. You get *all* the luck.'

Jasmin's nan liked to stop and chat to the neighbours on the way. 'By the time we get to Nan's, I've missed all the good cartoons on telly,' Jasmin grumbled.

'Yep,' said Carly, 'I'm lucky. I always do what I like, when I like.'

Some days, Carly dawdled along, staring in the shop windows. Other days, she raced down the pavement, overtaking people who got in her way, just to try and beat her own record. She didn't even stop for old ladies

with their shopping trolleys. She just barged past them, laughing.

'Tee hee hee!' she crowed. 'No one stands in my way.'

'Poor wee mite,' said Jasmin's nan. 'One of these days she'll cause an accident. And no one to take decent care of her.'

When other people reached home, their mums or dads or nans or childminders made them some tea, or a jam sandwich, or a chocolate milk-shake. Then they encouraged them to do sensible things, like riding their bikes, or jigsaw puzzles or playing with their baby brothers.

Carly didn't. Quite often she went home to an empty flat and picked at leftovers from the fridge. Then she ran up and down outside, buzzing on everybody else's front doorbells. She always got away before anybody answered, so they never knew who it was.

'Yep,' Carly agreed with Jasmin. 'I'm the luckiest person in the whole school. Nobody fusses after *me*!'

Even Carly's mum didn't get in her way, for she was either out or lying around feeling poorly.

But then, suddenly, without warning, everything changed.

2 A stranger at the gate

ON A HOT, sunny afternoon, instead of setting out for home, Carly was messing about in the cloakroom with the taps. She was trying to see if she could get the cold water to squirt right up over the coat-hooks.

She'd nearly managed it when Tony came jogging back into the cloakroom and began searching for his lost trainer.

'Hi, Carly!' he called.

'Hi,' said Carly. 'Watch out for the fountain.'

Tony's trainer was on the floor behind the radiator.

'Yuck, it's all wet!' he said when he finally found it.

'Only a bit,' said Carly. 'It'll dry off.'

'By the way,' said Tony. 'There's someone waiting for you by the gate.'

'*Course there isn't*,' said Carly. She knew it couldn't be her mum because when she last saw her, early this morning, she was feeling so rough she didn't even want a drink of water. And, besides, her mum never came to school if she could help it, except for the Christmas play. And there wasn't anybody else it could be.

'Suit yourself,' said Tony with a shrug. He put on his wet trainer and Carly went on squirting water. Next, Jasmin came running in, all out of breath.

'Oh, Carly, *here* you are! I've been looking for you everywhere. Someone's come to meet you, down at the gate.'

'I know, I know,' snapped Carly, because she didn't want Jasmin knowing that she hadn't a clue who it might be. She didn't want Jasmin bossing her about either. 'Tony's already told me.'

'Well, you'd better hurry. She's getting very impatient. Is she your auntie?'

'No, she is not!'

Carly did not, as far as she knew, have any aunties, unless they were in Trinidad.

By the time Carly had turned off all the taps and mopped up the water with someone's left-behind pullover, the person who'd come to meet her had already reached the entrance hall and was talking to the teacher on duty. The visitor held a big leather brief-case under her arm and had an important plastic badge with her name on it pinned to her jacket.

It looked as though, from now on, things weren't going to be so hassle free.

Carly sauntered into the entrance hall as though she had all the time in the world. She read the visitor's badge. Then she said, 'Ms Yvonne Onions? You've come to see me? And how can I help you?'

'Ah,' said the lady to the teacher on duty. 'So this is Carlene. Well, Carlene, I think you will find that the boot is on the other foot. It is *I* who have come to help *you*.'

'But I don't need any help, ta all the same. I'll let you know if I do.'

Jasmin and Tony, who were listening, both giggled.

'No, Carlene, clearly you don't understand. I have some bad news for you.'

'Poor me. Gone and won the Lottery, have I?'

'It's your mother. She's been taken ill

and I'm afraid she's gone to hospital.'

Jasmin gasped. Carly was most surprised too, for although her mum often seemed very tired, she was never actually ill. But she certainly didn't want this Ms Onions, or the teacher, or Jasmin, or Tony, or Jasmin's nan, or any of the others who'd gathered round in a nosy way, to know.

'That's all to the good then, isn't it?' she said. 'Best place for her if she's feeling poorly. Thanks for letting me know. I'd better be pushing off now.'

But Ms Onions wouldn't let her leave on her own. 'No, Carlene. You've got to come along with me,' she insisted. 'I'm taking you to stay with some nice people who will be your foster-parents.'

'D'you think I'm daft? I'm not going with you! I'm heading straight home, just like my mum always tells me I must,' said Carly. It had just occurred to her that if her mum was really going to be away for the night, she could stay up and watch telly till late, maybe right through till the scary films after midnight.

Unfortunately, the teacher on duty agreed with Ms Onions.

'No, Carly love,' she said. 'You can't go back to an empty flat. It just wouldn't do. But it won't be for long, I'm sure.'

Jasmin, who was still listening, said to Tony, 'Fancy her being allowed to go off when it's not even holidays yet. It's just not fair. Carly always gets all the fun.'

Ms Onions' car was parked on the street outside school. Carly was allowed to sit in the front. Ms Onions checked that the seatbelt was securely fixed, almost as though Carly wasn't old enough to see to it herself.

As they drove off, Carly waved back at Jasmin and Tony and the others standing outside school as though she was the

Queen. But, inside, she felt strange and rather scared.

At the traffic-lights, Carly said, 'Won't I need some things?' She was sure that most people took a suitcase with them when they went away, even when it was only for one night.

'Yes, Carlene,' said Ms Onions. 'I popped back to your flat earlier. I've collected what you'll need. It's all in that bin-liner on the back seat.'

'Bit saucy, aren't you? Poking around in someone's flat when they're not in?'

'Your mother gave me the key.'

'I bet you've brought all the wrong stuff. I bet you packed my pink pyjamas with rabbits on. They're really gross. I hate pink.

Pink's for babies.'

Carly didn't want these foster people where she was going to stay to think she was still a baby.

'And another thing,' she said. 'Why d'you have to keep calling me Carlene? Everybody knows I'm Carly.'

3 *At the house of the Bears*

'I'M GOING TO be sick!' Carly shrieked. 'Probably quite soon.'

But Ms Onions wouldn't stop for anything. She just drove on and on till at last they reached a quiet suburb, far away. All the houses were in tidy rows. Each house had a garden. Each garden had a little gate. Carly had always wanted to live in a proper house like this, with a garden. She stopped thinking about being sick. She began to feel almost excited.

But she didn't want Ms Onions to know

what she felt. So she made a being-very-sick face, then gave the little white gate a quick kick.

'Now then, Carlene, nice behaviour if you can manage it,' said Ms Onions, glaring, before leading the way along the concrete path between neat beds planted with tidy red flowers in straight lines. She hurried up the well-swept front steps to the front door. Carly came slowly behind. Ms Onions rang the door chimes and while they waited, she tried to smile.

'It says in your notes that you were last taken into care when your parents separated. But you were only little, so I don't expect you remember?'

Carly scowled. 'Course I remember. I

didn't like it then, so I don't know why anyone thinks I'm going to like it any better this time.'

'Mr and Mrs McVitie want to be your friends.'

'How can they be when I haven't even met them yet? I thought children weren't supposed to talk to strangers.'

Ms Onions sighed. 'Well, Mr and Mrs McVitie are very kind people, so I just hope you'll try to be cooperative.'

'Taking their time, aren't they? I haven't got all day to stand around waiting,' said Carly, and she leaned her elbow on the door chimes and kept it there. The chimes inside clanged and clanged like a fire engine.

The front door finally opened. Two short, fat people waddled forward with their arms outstretched in welcome.

They were both beaming. Carly stared. They were too middle-aged to be *any-body*'s parents, even foster ones.

'Ah,' said Ms Onions. 'Mr and Mrs McVitie.'

'And who is the sweet young miss you've brought us today, Miss Onions?' beamed Mr McVitie.

'A very noisy and opinionated girl,' said Ms Onions sourly. She handed Mr McVitie the black bin-liner with Carly's things in it, and a form to fill in.

'On the dotted line, at the bottom, please, Mr McVitie,' said Ms Onions. 'It's just to say you've got her.'

'Why, what a dear wee poppet!' said Mrs McVitie, wrapping her short, chubby arms round Carly. It felt good, like being hugged by a soft, cuddly teddy. But Carly wasn't going to let *them* know that.

'Yuk! I just hate smoochy old-timers,' she muttered and pulled herself roughly away so that Mrs McVitie staggered backwards and bumped into the door chimes which started clanging all over again.

Ms Onions wouldn't stop long enough even for a cup of tea, though the McVities offered her one.

As she watched Ms Onions' car speeding

away down the street, Carly felt as though she was a cumbersome parcel that had been successfully delivered.

'So you're fond of noise, eh?' said Mr McVitie, patting Carly on the head. 'That's great. I'm a bit of a spin doctor myself. Maybe we can get hep together?'

He had a friendly, furry face, almost like Father Christmas.

'Push over,' Carly snarled, 'you're so old you couldn't even swing on a Zimmer frame.'

'Oh, this is going to be such fun!' Mrs McVitie laughed, clapping her fat hands. 'I just know we're all going to get on like a house on fire. I think you'd better call us Auntie Heather and Uncle Dougal. Now, dear, let me show you your room, while Uncle Dougal puts on the kettle.'

'You're not my aunt and he's not my uncle,' said Carly. 'I'm going to call you the Bears. Because that's what you look like. A fat bear and a grizzly bear.'

Mrs McVitie seemed quite pleased with the idea of becoming a fat bear. 'And I expect you're going to be the baby bear?'

'Not likely.'

'Goldilocks?' suggested Mr McVitie.

'Course not. That's just stupid,' Carly said. 'The wolf, more like it.' Then, she thought, she could tear them both to pieces with her sharp fangs.

'I'm not staying here, you know,' she said. 'I'm probably going to run away. And you'll be held responsible.'

'Very well, dearie,' Mrs Fatty Bear agreed cheerfully.

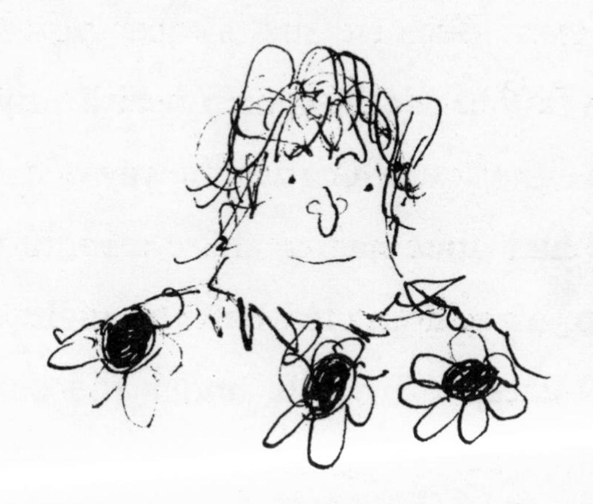

4 Home from home

'AND I'M NOT sharing with anyone either,' said Carly. 'No way.'

She had once had to share a room with Jasmin. They'd giggled half the night, and eaten digestive biscuits under the covers. Jasmin's nan had got a bit cross.

'I *hate* having to share.'

'Quite so, dearie,' said Mrs Fatty Bear kindly.

Carly's room was to be all her own. It had pretty pink curtains and its own pink wash basin in the corner with scented pink soap so new that it was still in its wrapper. There was a soft pink carpet on the floor and a pink lamp by the bed. It was such a beautiful room that Carly wished Jasmin could have been there to see it.

'Oh, it's truly gross!' she groaned.

'What's that, hen?' Mrs Fatty Bear was fetching some fluffy pink bath-towels from the airing cupboard, so she didn't hear properly. Carly had to complain again, louder.

'Never before have I had to sleep in such a poky hovel. And, yuk! Whoever chose this horrible pink must be related to a pig.'

At supper-time, which Mrs Fatty Bear called High Tea, there were fish fingers, chips, tomatoes and carrots, followed by blackberry and apple pie with fruit salad and cream.

Carly made sure that quite a lot of the cream, and some bits of tomato went on the floor.

'And there's scones, Abernethy farls and flapjacks to fill the gaps. And if you tell us your favourite food, hen, we'll do our best to make it for you, won't we, Uncle Dougal?'

'That's the ticket, Auntie Heather,' agreed Old Grizzly Bear, giving Carly a big wink as though they were already old pals. 'Round here, we aim to please.'

So, the next morning, when Mrs Fatty Bear handed Carly a bowlful of something she'd prepared for breakfast, Carly said, 'Yeeeergh. I never have *this* at home! What

is it?' She prodded it with the spoon, then pushed the bowl away even though she was hungry and the pale-brown stuff looked quite tasty.

'That's porridge, my little dearie,' said Mrs Fatty Bear.

Carly guessed it might be, because she'd seen something like it before, round at Jasmin's nan's place.

Mrs Fatty Bear brought out a dish of thick, fresh cream and a jar of honey to go with the porridge.

'Can't eat mucky-yuck like this,' said Carly. 'And, anyway, it's not what I have at home.'

At home, she had cereal without milk if there wasn't any milk. Or milk without cereal when there wasn't any cereal. Sometimes, if her mum hadn't been shopping, she didn't have any breakfast at all.

'Ah well,' said Mrs Fatty Bear with a smile. 'Just do your best with it for the time being.'

Carly slapped her spoon up and down in her bowl till little blobs splatted out in all directions and stuck wherever they landed like school glue. But the Bears took no notice.

'If bears eat porridge for breakfast, I wonder what young wolves eat for dinner,' said Old Grizzly Bear.

'Black-pudding. Made with fresh pig's blood,' snarled Carly, and she joggled the table with her feet so that when Mrs Fatty Bear picked up the teapot to pour out the tea, it went everywhere except into the cups.

'Black-pudding, hm? Splendid,' said Mrs Fatty Bear, mopping up the spilt tea and porridge blobs. 'I'll see if we can get some.'

'Only on Sundays,' said Carly quickly. 'Mostly, my mum cooks fufu and plantain and callaloo stew.'

In fact, it was her dad who used to cook fufu, plantain and callaloo stew. But he'd been gone so long that Carly couldn't remember what callaloo stew tasted like, let alone whether she'd liked it. As for her mum, she hadn't cooked a meal for ages. She was always too tired. Even opening a tin of beans was sometimes too much for her.

Mrs Fatty Bear looked doubtful. 'I'm not sure if Auntie Heather and Uncle Dougal can find *all* the ingredients for callaloo stew today. Our local shopkeeper is none too adventurous.'

'But when we tell him about our very

special guest, I'm sure he'll do his best to find us the things we need,' said Old Grizzly Bear. 'Callaloo stew! Yummy. I can't wait.' He rubbed his tummy and smacked his lips.

While the Bears were washing up, Carly poured salt into the sugar basin and shook pepper into the jam pot. Then she went and made rude faces at the goldfish swimming round in its glass tank.

When the Bears started getting down all their recipe books and looking up *Recipes of the World*, Carly wished she'd told them that her favourite food was something she really liked. She should have said chips and beans and strawberries and chocolate-chip ice-cream.

‘The important thing,’ said Mrs Fatty Bear, ‘is that you should feel at home.’

‘Home from home,’ Old Grizzly Bear agreed.

So Carly slammed doors, just like she did at home, and she zapped the TV from channel to channel with the volume on full. She picked at food in the fridge and she left the freezer door open.

But it still didn’t *feel* like living at home. For one thing, the Bears stayed quite calm and went on doing everything in their same tidy way. They always got up at the same time. They fed their goldish at the same time. They washed up the dishes at the same time and in the same order. They told Carly the same merry tales about the mischievous pranks of the other girls and boys who had been sent by Ms Onions to stay with them. And they always seemed to be cheerful. Even when Carly trampled on the flowerbeds, then came in and lay on their clean settee and put her muddy trainers on the cushions, Mrs Fatty Bear went on smiling.

'It might be a good idea, Carly poppet,' she said as she followed the trail of earth through the house, 'if you take your trainers off if they're very dirty.'

'No,' said Carly. 'Why should I?' And she ground the heels hard into the cushion covers.

On the second day, Mrs Fatty Bear explained quietly and carefully what was wrong with Carly's mum. She had an illness that was quite serious and very infectious.

'That's why Miss Onions and the doctors have decided that it's best for you not to see her, otherwise you may catch it too.'

'What about the nurses?' said Carly. 'Don't suppose they want to be catching my mum's horrible germs either.'

'I daresay they wear masks,' said Mrs Fatty Bear. Later, she explained that they wouldn't know for a while if Carly had the infection too, so it would be best if she was kept away from other children for the time being.

'That's fine by me. Because I hate other children,' said Carly, even though sometimes thinking about Jasmin made Carly feel sad with missing her.

'It's only for a short while. To be on the safe side. You certainly seem to be as fit as a merry fiddle, don't you, dearie? Maybe you'd like to lend a hand with the drying-up?' Mrs Fatty Bear offered Carly a tea-cloth.

‘Not likely,’ said Carly. ‘That’s your job.’ And she shoved the tea-cloth back into Mrs Fatty Bear’s hand.

Sometimes, thinking about her mum, surrounded by nurses wearing masks, made Carly feel like crying. Sometimes she just felt like screaming for no reason at all.

So Carly decided it was best not to let herself think too much about her mum, not about the sad, lonely bits when Mum was out and the flat was empty, nor about the bits when Mum was there but feeling cross and poorly. As for the good bits, Carly couldn’t remember if there were any.

Within a short time, she was surprised to find that she was beginning to like living with the Bears. It felt safe, always knowing what was going to happen next. However hard Carly tried to upset things, nothing ever changed too much. She liked being allowed to feed the goldfish in the morning with a tiny pinch of its food flakes, and being able to help Old Grizzly Bear water the red flowers in the garden in the evening with the big green can, which you filled at an outside tap beside the shed. She liked the way Mrs Fatty Bear read her stories out of books and the way Old Grizzly Bear played snap with her in the evening. She liked having her own friendly pink room, with its washbasin and pink scented soap. She liked the meals, except for the time she put three spoonfuls of sugar in her tea because she'd forgotten she had put salt in the sugar bowl to trick the Bears.

Even the spicy callaloo stew the two Bears had cooked turned out to be quite good, though Carly didn't tell them so because she knew it was safer never to say thank you for anything.

Carly was just beginning to think she could go on living like this for ever, and that maybe she'd give up slamming doors and wiping her muddy trainers on the cushions when suddenly, without any warning, something went and happened to change it all again.

A letter arrived in the post. It was for Carly.

5 The letter

SEEING THE ENVELOPE, there on the Bears' kitchen table, propped up against the honey jar, put Carly in a wobbly, upset mood. The letter was from her mum. She recognised the writing.

Carly didn't want to have to start thinking about her mum right now. She knew it would spoil everything.

So she sprinkled brown sugar, as thick as sand on the beach, all over the porridge that Mrs Fatty Bear gave her. Then she poured on some honey, and Mrs Fatty

Bear plopped a nice fat dollop of double cream on top. Carly had got used to the Bears' breakfasts. She even enjoyed them. They made getting up in the morning seem quite nice, especially as nobody told her to hurry up or she'd be late for school.

Carly ate her porridge slowly, one spoonful at a time, feeling her appetite fade away.

'Aren't you going to open your nice letter, my little dearie?' asked Mrs Fatty Bear.

'No,' growled Carly. 'Anyway, how d'you know it's nice? It's probably horrible.' If it was from her mum it was probably full of germs, too. Whatever it said, it was bound to interfere with her life.

'Very well, dear,' said Mrs Fatty Bear.

After she'd fed the goldfish, Carly took the letter upstairs to her pink bedroom to read on her own.

It went like this:

Dear Carly,

How is life treating you with the foster people?

I hope they are all right to you. I'll be seeing you Saturday when the social worker brings you over. I'm safe to visit now. Take care.

Love and hugs from Mum.

Carly was glad she hadn't opened the letter downstairs.

She didn't want the Bears to see her mum's funny writing with the lines all sloping sideways down to one corner of the paper. It looked as though she'd written it lying flat on her back, it was so messy.

Most of all, Carly didn't want them to see that her mum was expecting her to go and visit.

So Carly sat in her pink bedroom for a long time, flicking the bedside lamp on and off till she had an idea. If she got rid of the letter, the Bears wouldn't have to know what it said.

Carly scrumpled the paper up into a ball, then wondered where to put it. She searched all over the room for a good hiding-place. If she put it under her mattress, Mrs Fatty Bear would be sure to find it when she made the bed. If she put it in the chest of drawers, Mrs Fatty Bear would see it when she put away Carly's clean clothes. If she threw it out of the window Old Grizzly Bear would see it lying on the concrete path looking untidy.

She thought of the washbasin. It had a

small, dark plug-hole where the water ran away. No one would ever think of looking down there. So she pushed in the letter, then scrumpled up the envelope too, and shoved that into the other hole at the top of the basin where the water ran away if you filled the bowl too full. After that, she felt much better and had a really nice morning.

She skipped downstairs and went out to watch Old Grizzly Bear doing things in the garden. She watered the red flowers several times over. She played in the apple tree. She talked to the goldfish. Then she went for a walk in the woods with Old Grizzly Bear to look for wild bees making wild honey. They didn't find any bees, but they found some damsons instead and, soon,

Carly had managed to make herself forget all about her mum's letter.

By the time she and Old Grizzly Bear got back from their walk they were both feeling hungry and ready to enjoy their dinner.

'It's kedgeree today,' said Old Grizzly Bear. 'With green beans, salad and sausages to fill the gaps, and trifle and custard afterwards.'

Carly wasn't sure about the kedgeree but she thought she'd give it a try.

But when they got in, there was no dinner ready.

This was most unusual. The Bears always had their meals on time. Instead, Mrs Fatty Bear was wearing her rubber galoshes indoors. The dining table was covered in wet cloths and the goldfish was looking miserable in a saucepan of water on the draining board.

'Just a little bit of a flood,' said Mrs Fatty Bear brightly. 'Nothing serious. No need to build an ark.'

The flood was in the sitting-room. The settee was soggy. So was the carpet upstairs in Carly's room. Water was still dripping down through the ceiling.

'Luckily, most of it went into the fish

tank,' said Mrs Fatty Bear smiling. 'Very useful having the fish tank right there.'

Carly didn't usually feel sorry for anybody. But for a moment she felt almost sad for the goldfish, first having dirty water

dripping into its tank, then being moved into a dark saucepan which it couldn't see out of.

And she was surprised that the Bears, who liked things so tidy, didn't seem put out by all the mess. Even having their

dinner half an hour late didn't seem to upset them. They both took it as an excuse to eat twice as much and then went on chatting as cheerfully as usual.

'Not to worry,' said Old Grizzly Bear. 'I'll soon have everything back to normal.'

After dinner he put on his big, baggy blue overalls, which made him look like a plumber, and stomped upstairs with some rods and hammers and spanners. First he pulled up the pink carpet so that it could dry. Then he poked down the pipes with his long rods till he fished out some bits of wet paper.

'Well, blow me over!' he said. 'So that's what's been blocking things up and causing the trouble!'

'Ooh what a shame!' said Mrs Fatty Bear. 'It's wee Carly's letter. It must have been blown into the basin by the breeze.'

She tried to flatten it out. 'And now all the writing's washed out. So we'll never know what it said.'

Mr and Mrs Bear both looked so sad, yet calm, standing there on their sodden floor trying to read the wet letter, that Carly felt quite upset for them.

Then she wondered why they didn't yell

and throw things, like Mum had that time when Carly let the washing-up bowl overflow. She wondered if perhaps it was because Mr and Mrs Bear liked her anyway, just the way she was, whatever she did.

She suddenly felt like telling the truth, or a little bit of the truth.

'But I do know what it says,' she said in a small voice. 'Because, you see, I just had time to read it before it blew itself down the plug-hole. It says I've got to go and visit Mum. Tomorrow.'

'Well, isn't that just fine!' said Mrs Fatty Bear, beaming happily, almost as though she'd known all along. 'In that case, you'll be wanting to look your best. So how about

I run the iron over your best dress tonight? And we'd better shampoo your hair at bath-time. And find you some clean socks.'

'And I'll polish your shoes,' added Old Grizzly Bear.

Already, the Bears seemed to have completely forgotten about the flood. They were much more interested in helping Carly get ready for her outing.

By next morning, the carpets were nearly dry and only a bit smelly, and the fish was safely back in its own clean tank.

After breakfast, Old Grizzly Bear picked a big bunch of his very best red flowers from the garden, though from the back of the beds where it wouldn't spoil the straight lines so much. Then he chose one of the biggest jars of golden honey from his shed.

'That's for you to take to your mother,' he said proudly, polishing the glass on his apron. 'A spoonful a day to keep ill-health away.' He tied the bouquet of flowers with some raffia.

'You'll give her our very best wishes, won't you, dear?' said Mrs Fatty Bear.

'Maybe,' said Carly uncertainly.

Ms Onions arrived in her blue car to fetch Carly at ten thirty on the dot.

Ms Onions smiled and said, 'Good morning, Carlene. I've had to give up my day off to drive out here so I hope you've decided to be in a better mood than last time.'

Carly narrowed her eyes like an enraged wolf.

6 The man with the broken leg

CARLY HAD TO trail along behind Ms Onions right through the hospital and Ms Onions had to ask three times before they even found the right ward. Carly's mum was in a high bed at the far end. She was propped up against some pillows. She had on her tired face, as if she'd just washed the kitchen floor, then emptied the bins, then been down to the launderette and back. In fact, all she was doing was lying there, not moving.

Even though Mrs Fatty Bear had

warned Carly that the illness might have made her mum go a bit yellow-looking, it was still a bad surprise to see her.

Carly stared. The woman lying there didn't even look like her mum. She looked like a colouring-in picture that had gone wrong. Her face was yellow. So were her hands, her neck, her cheeks and her eyeballs. And when she smiled at Carly, even her smile seemed a bit yellow. The only things that weren't yellow were her teeth and her nightgown.

'Go on then, Carlene,' said Ms Onions, sitting down on the chair beside the bed. 'Say hello to your mother nicely. Tell her how much you've been looking forward to coming and seeing her.'

Carly's mum couldn't sit up by herself, but she held out her hand. It was so thin it looked to Carly more like a chicken's claw than a real hand.

'Hi, mum,' said Carly. 'Flowers and honey. Do you good. The fat Bears where I'm staying said so.' She dumped the bouquet and the glass jar on the bed by her mum's feet. 'I don't think I'll kiss you because whatever you've got might be catching.'

'Not any more,' said her mum with a faint smile. 'I'm getting better every day.'

'You don't look it,' said Carly.

After a bit, Carly's mum closed her eyes.

And Carly couldn't think of anything else useful to say.

She didn't like being here. To pass the time, she snapped the heads off some of the red flowers and she dipped her finger in the honey. Then she went outside and walked up and down the corridor, while Ms Onions talked to her mum.

Carly found some other patients to look at. They had much safer things wrong with them. They didn't look so poorly either. Carly saw a man with a broken leg who had a very interesting crane over his bed for his leg to go up and down on. He seemed to be having a great time. He had his mates round him and lots of crisps and cans of ginger beer.

Back in Ms Onions' car, Carly said, 'I wish my mum had a broken leg.'

'Really!' snapped Ms Onions. 'What a cruel thing for a girl to say about her own mother!'

Ms Onions didn't understand. Carly had meant she wished her mum had a broken leg *instead* of being yellow, not as well as. But it wasn't worth trying to explain anything to Ms Onions.

'Everyone's been bending over backwards on your account . . .' Ms Onions went on.

'*I* haven't seen anybody doing any bending,' Carly muttered.

'. . . and all you can do in return for our support is to say these terrible things. It's just not good enough!' Ms Onions snorted.

Carly ground her back teeth together. If she'd been a real wolf, she'd have leapt at Ms Onions' throat and savaged her into tiny pieces.

7 The vow of silence

CARLY SO MUCH wanted it to be all right when she got back to the Bears' tidy life. But somehow she knew it wouldn't be, especially if they started asking her loads of questions.

Old Grizzly Bear was trimming grass in the garden to make the path edges even straighter. Mrs Fatty Bear was in the kitchen making currant scones that were all just the right size and shape. They both welcomed her back as though she'd been away for years instead of just half a day.

'And so how is our little traveller?' asked

Mrs Fatty Bear. 'I'm planning on cooking fufu and fried plantain tonight, with a blackberry and apple pie to follow – if that meets your fancy, hen?'

Old Grizzly Bear paused from his garden tidying to tell Carly how he'd been inventing a brand-new card game while she was out, especially for her. 'It's like snap, only much better,' he said, with a merry twinkle in his eye. 'We'll have a go after High Tea, shall we, my dear?'

'I'm afraid I don't play cards any more,' said Carly stiffly. 'It's too babyish. But thank you for thinking of me.'

She did so want to seem pleased to be back. But somehow she couldn't when she knew they were going to start asking

difficult questions.

During tea they began, just like she knew they would.

'And how was your journey, dear? Not too long, I hope? Did you suck the barley-sugar I gave you to stop you feeling sick?'

Carly nodded.

'And your mother? How was she? I'll bet she was pleased to see you, wasn't she?'

'Sort of,' Carly mumbled.

'And the flowers. Did she like them?' asked Old Grizzly Bear. 'I expect you told her how you helped grow them, didn't you?'

'Miss Onions says she's coming along very well. Only a week or two more in the hospital, then she'll be ready to have a little holiday to get quite over it, and then she'll be home. That'll be exciting, won't it?'

Carly wanted to shout very loudly, No. No. NO! Why do you have to keep pestering me with these questions? I don't know. I don't know. I don't know! But instead it came out very quietly.

'I don't really know anything. But there's something I've got to tell you both. I've made an important decision. I have taken a vow of silence. I'm not going to be able to speak to anybody.'

'A vow of silence, eh?' said Old Grizzly Bear. 'That's a big step.'

'Oh my,' said Mrs Fatty Bear, 'what a shame. So we'll be missing the sound of your merry voice for a wee while.'

Carly nodded. 'For ever.'

'Now why, I wonder, should you wish to be doing that?'

Carly shrugged. She didn't know why. If only she did, she thought, everything would be easy. She just knew that she felt upset. She didn't have any answers.

When the meal was over, she helped clear the table without saying a word. She helped with the drying-up without even being asked. She carried the empty milk bottles out to the front step.

Finally, she nodded a silent goodnight to the two Bears and wearily climbed the stairs to her room. She got into bed and pulled the eiderdown over her head.

'Horrible covers,' she muttered silently. 'Pink as a pig's bottom.'

She lay and thought sad, bad thoughts about how she was the unluckiest person in the whole world. And she hardly slept a wink all night.

7 Carly's tears

IN THE MORNING, Carly stayed under the covers with the curtains drawn. The vow of silence was a terrible burden. When you couldn't talk, there was no point in getting up.

She listened to the Bears being busy downstairs. There was a clatter of pans and lots of crockery-rattling as the table was laid. Then came the smells of creamy porridge, sizzly bacon, buttered eggs and toasting muffins.

After a while she heard Mrs Fatty Bear

calling up the stairs.

'Cooeee, Carly my dear! Breakfast's ready when you are!'

But Carly couldn't shout anything back. She just had to go on lying there in the half-dark while they were enjoying themselves.

Later on, Carly heard Old Grizzly Bear go pottering out to the garden shed and Mrs Fatty Bear begin some noisy baking. As the morning dragged slowly on, Carly grew hungrier and lonelier.

Then there was a new sound, a slow wheezing and clumping coming up the stairs. It was Mrs Fatty Bear. Carly heard the bedroom door open.

'Hello there, my little sleepy-head!'

Carly took no notice.

'Would you fancy a wee bite of elevenses, just to keep your strength up? Uncle Dougal thought you might be feeling peckish by now, you poor wee mite.'

Carly kept her head under the eider-down as Mrs Fatty Bear chattered on. 'So here's a nice mug of hot chocolate and a slice or two of fresh ginger cake.'

Mrs Fatty Bear put the tray where Carly could reach it, opened the curtains and sat heavily down on the edge of Carly's bed, right where Carly's feet were.

'I was wondering,' she said, 'what all this sadness is about? Maybe you could let me share it with you? By the way, won't you try a crumb of the ginger cake? It's really turned out very well.'

Carly poked her head out. 'Why d'you have to keep talking and talking at me like this? Don't you understand? I've taken a vow because I don't want to have to speak to you, or to anybody, ever again.'

Mrs Fatty Bear merely settled her fat bottom more comfortably on to the middle of the bed so that Carly had to move her feet right over to the other side.

'Quite so, my dear. But *I* haven't made any vows of silence, have I now? And I suspect, my little dearie, that you don't want to talk because you're unhappy inside.'

'No I'm not,' snapped Carly.

'Maybe you're missing your pals? Maybe you're worried about what's going to happen to you next?'

Yes, thought Carly, she *was* worried about that. But how did Mrs Fatty Bear know?

'Perhaps you're anxious because you had to look after your mum so much? Especially when she got so poorly. Maybe you've had to look after her more than she ever looked after you?'

Carly sniffed.

'And maybe you're upset because people you don't like very much come and boss you about and make decisions without asking you first?'

Carly thought of Ms Onions.

'But however cruel they seem, they're only ordinary folk doing their job as well as they can to make sure you come to no harm.'

Mrs Fatty Bear's voice was warm and friendly, like a talking teddy when you turned it upside down. Carly liked listening to her. It was almost like hearing the story of her own life being told.

'Your mum's been getting ill for quite some time. You had to live with it. You were very courageous, managing as well as you did. I don't suppose anybody's ever thought to tell you that.'

Carly felt something trickling down the side of her nose. She didn't know how it got there. Although she often yelled or shouted, she wasn't soppy. She never cried. Mrs Fatty Bear wiped the tear away with her pudgy hand.

Old Grizzly Bear came stumping upstairs. He peered round the door. 'Now then, Auntie Heather,' he said, 'what's all this? I thought you had come to cheer her up, not to make her cry.'

Carly thought how, in a funny kind of a way, Mrs Fatty Bear *had* begun to cheer her up.

9 The picture postcards

MRS FATTY BEAR announced that dinner was to be at a different time from usual, twenty-five minutes early.

'We can't have our little Carly looking half starved, can we now, Uncle Dougal?'

Old Grizzly Bear agreed.

On account of Carly not having had any breakfast, there were even more choices of things to eat than usual.

There were fish fingers, mixed green salad, smoked kippers, chips, lasagne, creamed potatoes, grilled tomatoes, haddock paté, and mushroom and oyster pie.

'Made with oysters fresh from Loch Fyne,' said Old Grizzly Bear.

'And to follow,' said Mrs Fatty Bear, 'we've got honey mousse and blackberry ice-cream. With some nice wee shortbread fingers to fill the gaps.'

The Bears ate several extra big helpings of everything.

'It's to keep you company, my dearie,' explained Mrs Fatty Bear. 'We wouldn't want you to feel you were eating on your own.'

One day, Carly thought, they'll grow so fat that they won't be able to move.

But she was trying to be nice, so she decided not to say anything about healthy diets.

Instead, she said, 'Thank you Auntie Heather and Uncle Dougal for cooking such a nice meal. I feel much better already.'

'Well, hen,' said Mrs Fatty Bear, 'things don't usually get better overnight, but little by little. Especially when you air your worries and make a plan for the future.'

'Oh good,' said Carly. 'Because I've got a plan. I think I should stay here with you until I'm grown up. That'd be best, wouldn't it? And, of course, from now on I'll always be as good as gold.'

She was surprised that, instead of being pleased, both the Bears slowly shook their heads.

'No, dearie,' said Mrs Fatty Bear firmly. 'I'm afraid that wouldn't be right.'

'No, not the ticket at all,' agreed Old Grizzly Bear.

'But why not?' said Carly. 'I'll always do exactly what you ask me to, honest. *Please*?'

Mrs Fatty Bear said, 'We can never be your proper, permanent parents.'

Old Grizzly Bear said, 'Because, you see, we're only fat, middle-aged foster bears. And rather dull sticks at that.'

'Besides,' added Mrs Fatty Bear, 'your own mother needs you, just as you need her.'

Old Grizzly Bear agreed and kept nodding his furry head up and down as though it were on a spring. 'That's right. Wolves live in packs. They stick together.'

'But if you send me away, I'll *miss* you,' Carly said.

'Of course you will, hen. And we'll miss you too. But I daresay you could come and visit us.'

'That's right,' said Old Grizzly Bear, giving Carly a friendly pat on the shoulder so that she nearly choked on the honey mousse. 'You must bring your mother to stay. We'd like to meet her.'

'Here?' said Carly. The idea of her mum

being in the same place as the Bears felt odd.

'What about next holidays? For a long weekend?'

'But how would we get here?' It had taken ages in Ms Onions' car.

Old Grizzly Bear said, 'On the bus, of course. That'd be the 103, from the city centre. Then change at Green Wood Garage. On to the 244B. It'd be quite an adventure for the two of you.'

At first, Carly couldn't think that she'd ever been on any nice outings with her mum. But then she remembered how, long ago, before her mum started being so tired, they used to go to the swings in the park together, or wander round the shops, or sit under the bridge in the rain and eat chips. She wondered if it would ever be like that again.

'Auntie Heather,' she said, 'if my mum stayed, would you cook porridge for her breakfast, like you do for me?'

'I believe that could be arranged. What do you think, Uncle Dougal?'

'Yes, I'm sure we could manage that.'

Carly began to feel almost hopeful. 'And could you teach Mum how to do it so she could make it for me at home?'

They both thought that could be arranged too.

After dinner, Mrs Fatty Bear said it was high time to write to Carly's mum. She gave Carly a bundle of postcards to choose from and Carly picked a pretty picture of some mountains and lakes.

Dear Mum,

Having a lovely time.

But looking forward to seeing you again when you get back from your nursing home and I get back from Auntie Heather and Uncle Dougal's.

Love, Carly.

She chose a card for Jasmin too.

Hi there!

Having a brill time here.

Be back soon. Say hi to Tony and to Miss Wright from me. Also to your nan.

Here's a joke: why did the owl howl? Because the woodpecker would peck her.

Ha ha. See if Tony can get it.

From Carly xxx

PS The kisses aren't for Tony.

No way.

Carly and Mr and Mrs McVitie walked down the road to the postbox together. When they got back, Mrs McVitie thought it was time for another little something to eat.

'I don't know about you,' she said, 'but I'm as hungry as a wolf.'

And she got out the biscuit barrel, and the cake tin, and the honey pot, and some walnut scones, and the jam and the cheese and the pickles and the fruit and a few muffins and some tomato relish and the chocolate sauce and a few tea-cakes and . . .

If you enjoyed reading this book, you might like to try another story from the MAMMOTH READ series:

Name Games Theresa Breslin
The Chocolate Touch Patrick Skene Catling
The Chocolate Touch II Patrick Skene Catling
Dead Trouble Keith Gray
Fireball and the Hero Douglas Hill
The Gargoyle Garry Kilworth
My Frog and I Jan Mark
Ghost Blades Anthony Masters
How's Harry? Steve May
The Marble Crusher Michael Morpurgo
Delilah Alone Jenny Nimmo
Seth and the Strangers Jenny Nimmo
Hurricane Summer Robert Swindells
Charlie's Champion Chase Hazel Townson

Mr Biff the Boxer

by ALLAN AHLBERG

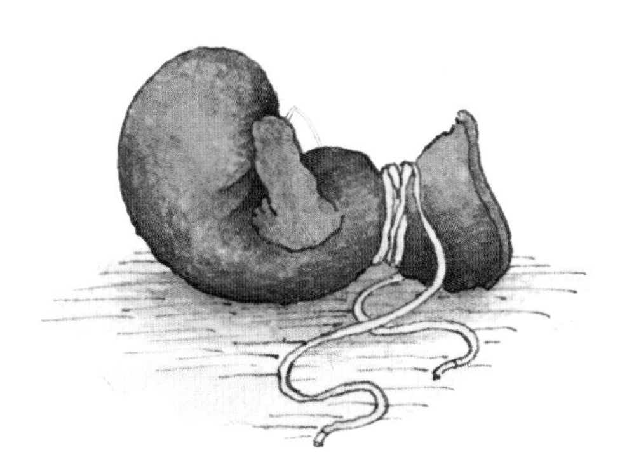

with pictures by
JANET AHLBERG

PUFFIN

PUFFIN BOOKS

Published by the Penguin Group
Penguin Books Ltd, 80 Strand, London WC2R 0RL, England
Penguin Group (USA), Inc., 375 Hudson Street, New York, New York 10014, USA
Penguin Books Australia Ltd, 250 Camberwell Road, Camberwell, Victoria 3124, Australia
Penguin Books Canada Ltd, 10 Alcorn Avenue, Toronto, Ontario, Canada M4V 3B2
Penguin Books India (P) Ltd, 11 Community Centre, Panchsheel Park, New Delhi – 110 017, India
Penguin Group (NZ), cnr Airborne and Rosedale Roads, Albany, Auckland 1310, New Zealad
Penguin Books (South Africa) (Pty) Ltd, 24 Sturdee Avenue, Rosebank 2196, South Africa

Penguin Books Ltd, Registered Offices: 80 Strand, London WC2R 0RL, England

www.penguin.com

First published by Viking 1980
Published in Puffin Books 1980
27 29 30 28 26

Educational Advisory Editor: Brian Thompson

Set in Century Schoolbook by Filmtype Services Limited, Scarborough
Manufactured in China

British Library Cataloguing in Publication Data
A CIP catalogue record for this book is available from the British Library

ISBN 0–140–31236–6

There was once a man named Mr Bop.
Mr Bop was a boxer.
He was as fit as a fiddle.
He was the toughest man in the town.
He was the champion.
There was another boxer in the town.
His name was Mr Biff.

Mr Biff was not as fit as a fiddle.
He ate too many cream cakes.
He drank too many bottles of beer.
Mr Biff was not tough.
He liked to sit in an easy chair
by a cosy fire.
He liked to put his slippers on
and read the paper.
He slept in a feather bed.

One day posters appeared in
the town. They said:

BIG CHARITY FIGHT

MR BIFF AGAINST MR BOP

Mr Biff told his wife
about the fight.
"It's for charity," he said.
"Me against Mr Bop."
"Oh dear," said Mrs Biff.
"They say he is the toughest man
in the town."
"They say his wife is the toughest
woman, too," said Mr Biff.

Mrs Biff told the children
about the fight.
"It's for charity," she said.
"Your dad against Mr Bop."
"Our dad will win," said Billy Biff.
"He will biff him!" Betty Biff said.

"But your dad is not fit,"
said Mrs Biff. "And he is not tough."
"We will be his trainers then,"
said Billy Biff.
"And toughen him up," Betty Biff said.
"You wait and see!"

The next day Mr Biff began training.
His family helped.
Billy Biff took him running.
Betty Biff took him skipping.

Mrs Biff hid his paper
and his slippers.
Bonzo Biff kept him out of
the easy chair.

The children also helped
to toughen him up.

Mrs Biff helped
to toughen him up too.

Mr Biff was put on a diet.
"I'd like three cream cakes
and a bottle of beer," he said.
"You can have three carrots
and a glass of water,"
said Mrs Biff.

Each day the children said,
"How do you feel, dad?"
Each day Mr Biff said,
"I feel terrible!"

But one day the children said,
"How do you feel, dad?"
And Mr Biff said,
"I feel as fit as a fiddle!"

Now it was the day of the fight.
A big tent was put up in the town.
Everybody was excited.
Crowds gathered.

The referee stepped into the ring.
"My lords, ladies and gentlemen,"
he said.
"On my right – Mr Bop!"
Everybody cheered.
"That's my husband!" said Mrs Bop.
"On my left – Mr Biff!"
Everybody cheered again.
"That's my dad!" Billy Biff shouted.

The time-keeper rang his bell.
"Ding-ding!"
The fight began.

Mr Biff stepped forward.

Mr Bop stepped forward.

Mr Bop moved to the right.

Mr Biff moved to the left.

Suddenly Mr Bop bopped Mr Biff.
At the same time Mr Biff biffed
Mr Bop.
They biffed and bopped each other out!

"It's a draw!" the referee said.
The time-keeper rang his bell.
"Ding-ding!"
The fight was ended.

...nine, ten
OUT!
It's a draw

In the dressing-room Mr Biff said,
"How do you feel?"
"I feel terrible!" said Mr Bop.
"I think bopping people is silly."
"Biffing people is silly too,"
said Mr Biff.
Then Mr Bop said,
"I feel hungry as well.
I have been on a diet."
"Me too," said Mr Biff.

"I could just eat a cream cake now!"
"And a jam tart!" said Mr Bop.
"And fish and chips!" said Mr Biff.
"And roast chicken and potatoes
and peas, and bread and butter,
and a bottle of beer!" Mr Bop said.

So that evening the two families
went out for a big dinner.
Mrs Biff made friends with Mrs Bop.
The Biff children made friends
with the Bop children.

Say 'when'
Cheers!

Bonzo Biff shared a bone with
the Bop dog.
And a happy time was had by all.

The End